HIGHLAND ENEMY

LENA COCHRAN

LENA COCHRAN

CHAPTER 1

Scotland Highlands, Near Loch Awe, 1313

Ellen Bryan knew she'd been gone too long, and by now, her father would be wondering where she was. This was never a good thing, but at the moment, she couldn't quite bring herself to care.

The falling sun slanting through the tree canopy overhead sent a dappling pattern dancing over the trunks and along the trail in front of her. Tilly's head bobbed as she bent to inspect a curious patch of purple flowers, but Ellen gently tugged her dark grey mane, reminding her of their purpose. The horse snorted her displeasure, but obeyed grudgingly, trotting on.

Ellen supposed she should have put a bridle on, or even a saddle, since trekking through the woods was never exactly a smooth ride, but she so much preferred it this way. Besides, she couldn't bear to lock the bit between Tilly's poor teeth. Tilly was her best friend in this foreign land. Back in England, she'd had friends. Here, in Scotland, she had only her horse. The animal knew Ellen better than even her father did, of that Ellen had no doubt. She didn't need reins to steer the mare; as far as she was concerned, the two of them could practically read each other's minds.

The woods were the only place Ellen ever felt at home. She pictured the drafty, expansive castle she was supposed to think of as home and shuddered. Aside from the collection of servants and her father's men, she and her father were the only ones who lived there. She often felt dejected by the extra, empty space dwarfing her all the time. Her father thrived in it, but she, on the other hand, sought to escape it at every opportunity.

"What do you think, Tilly?" she mused aloud, gazing around at the trees, their green leaves appearing golden in the late afternoon glow permeating the woods. "Shall we stay here forever? We'll build a home near the stream and live off berries and nuts. I'll find you a variety of grassy clearings and rotate you to a new one every day. I'll have to steal some seeds from a farmer to plant a vegetable patch so I can grow you some carrots, of course. Or maybe the farmer will be kind and just lend the seeds to me, especially if I offer to bring him some of the grown carrots every once in a while."

Ellen's gaze adopted a dreamy cast as she stared into space, her thoughts drifting. "Maybe he'll be young. And handsome. He might only be a simple farmer, but in his spare time, he'll dream of sailing across the ocean. He'll have a little dingy that he'll take out every morning, and once we meet, he'll invite me to join him. We'll watch the sunrise over the water and pretend we're setting sail for the west. Somewhere new. Somewhere different. Who knows?" She shrugged her thin shoulders. "Maybe one day I'll actually go."

Ellen fell quiet. Tilly continued to walk, high-stepping over tipped logs and stray branches lying across the path. They were almost at the end of the trees, and once they crossed out of the woods and back into the heather, they'd spot the castle stronghold, looming over the fields. She wished it looked out over the sea instead, but the cliffs were in the opposite direction. Oh, to spend every day gazing out over the very sea she was dreaming of... Though she could give up the idea of ever setting sail across it. Her father had different plans for her future, that much she knew for certain, even if he never divulged his plans to her.

She sighed heavily. Her father had grown worse of late, even more surly, more harsh. More than once, he'd raised his hand to strike her, and she'd only been saved by the sudden appearance of a servant or housemaid.

Ellen tried to reclaim the magic of her dream for just a little longer, but it was already gone, slipping through her fingers. The thought of her father often caused that. The sunlight was also disappearing fast, and the shadows were lengthening too quickly. She had no choice but to head back. Her shoulders sank in resignation, and she gently pressed her heels to Tilly's side. The horse might not be a filly anymore, but she was still as spirited and spry as if she were years younger than her actual age of six. Ears flicking forward, the mare leapt into an eager canter, clearing the fallen logs easily.

Ellen leaned forward over her neck and closed her eyes—just for a minute—to feel the wind lift her hair and blow over her face. It was almost enough, for that single, precious minute, to make her believe she was free.

ELLEN SCRUBBED DOWN and stabled Tilly herself; she always sent the groom away. He still tried to take her horse from her every time, which only resulted in her shooing him off irritably. Honestly, shouldn't he have figured out by now that she preferred to take care of the mare herself?

Alone in the stables at last, Ellen snuck Tilly a sugar cube, once the horse was safely back in her stall. The dust-grey horse whickered, and Ellen smiled. "I'm late for dinner," she said, "Father won't be pleased."

Still, instead of going to change out of her riding skirts, she wrapped her arms around the horse and pressed her face into Tilly's warm neck. She breathed in the horse's scent, and decided, not for the first time, that she'd never smelled anything better in her life. After the woods and the seaside, the stable was her favourite place in the world. She loved the faint whiff of oats, hay, and saddle leather always lingering in the air. And horse, naturally. Nothing comforted her like the smell of a horse.

Planting a kiss on Tilly's nose, she rubbed her ears one last time, and stepped back. "See you tomorrow, Til. Don't miss me too much." With a last fleeting smile, she turned and headed down the straw-dusted aisle on her way to the castle.

Ellen had been out for hours, deliberately disobeying her father's direct order to be back before sunset, and if there was one thing Lord Bryan hated—more than the Scots, that is—it was being kept waiting.

Squaring her shoulders, she strode across the grounds toward the castle entrance, preparing for the worst. Whatever it might be this time, though, she was determined to meet it with her head held high.

CHAPTER 2

It was the cry of the horses that woke her, rather than the shouting.

Sitting bolt upright, Ellen whipped her head around to the window. The drapes were billowing as a blustery wind blew inside. She flung off her blanket and jumped out of bed. Barefoot, she dashed across the flagstones to the window, shoving the fabric aside even as they tried to tangle about her.

"...*my* country, *my* lands, *my* home! I told ye to go, and ye wouldn't listen!" a voice was hollering somewhere below. Frantically, Ellen scanned the dark grounds for the source. The moon wasn't full tonight. What there was of it was currently obscured behind a thick wall of clouds, making it impossible to see anything below her window. That is, until the food storage shed erupted in flames.

Ellen gasped, stumbling backwards in terror. Her hand went to her mouth. The drapes blew and twisted around her, but this time she didn't notice. Her eyes were glued to the shed, the thatch ablaze in just a matter of moments. Red and gold sparks danced against the canvas of the night sky as smoke spiraled upwards. All of their food stores....

A man darted into view. Silhouetted against the flames, he raised his fist, screaming up at the castle. Ellen ducked out of sight immediately, peering instead around the edge of the window, unable to help herself.

"Ye've taken what ain't yers, and I swear to ye, I will be takin' it back. This is only a warning. Ye dinnae want to ken what I'll try next!"

Ellen's eyes were enormous as she watched the man vanish back into the shadows behind the burning storage house. Where was he going? She listened to the horses scream, and her heart clenched in her chest. The fire wasn't close enough to the stable to share its flames, but still—no doubt the animals were panicking. She needed to get to them; she needed to comfort them. Her father kept all of his prize horses in there, not just Tilly. The thought of Tilly made fear claw up her throat. She turned to go, careless of the consequences if she went running out there, nightgown and all, while that crazy Scotsman was still at large. She heard doors bang open.

Doors. *The stable doors.* She would know that sound anywhere.

The horses' cries grew louder. She raced back to the window. The man she'd seen screaming words scurried about below. And then, before she could do anything to stop it, she watched in horror as one by one the horses broke free, galloping out of the stable, frenzied. They shied from the fire and went tearing across the grounds and out of sight, toward the woods. The man had opened all the stalls, and now stood outside the stable, slapping rumps, shouting, waving his hands, scaring them, setting them off.

Tilly emerged from the barn last. A desperate cry burst from Ellen's lips as she watched the terrified mare make a beeline for the safety of the trees, away from the fire and the crazy man. She bolted into the dark, even as Ellen screamed her name from the window, forgetting to keep out of sight.

The man paused in his shouts and looked up at her. At least, she thought he did. She couldn't be sure for he was hidden in shadow. But she didn't care if he saw her. She didn't care about anything except getting Tilly back.

That was when she heard the roar from below. Her father. He'd gathered his best men, and they were storming across the grounds, swords bared and brandished high. The intruder vanished. *Just like that.* Ellen watched him melt into the darkness as if he'd been born from it. Her father continued to lead his men, no doubt determined to hunt him down, while a different team of servants hastened to douse the flames scouring the storage house.

Whirling away from the window, Ellen took off for the door, throwing the bolt and shoving it open. Her bare feet slapped against the stone floor as she raced down the hallway beneath the high, arching ceiling. Everyone in the castle was awake, no doubt running about, trying to figure out what was happening. This was her chance. At the last second, she remembered to grab her cloak, swinging it over her nightgown, before mashing her feet into a pair of boots.

Slipping out the door that led into the gardens, she kept to the shadows so she wouldn't be spotted, and then squeezed through a break in the fence she'd discovered years ago. Free of the castle grounds, she broke into a run, flying across the rolling fields toward the woods. Toward Tilly, wherever she'd gone.

Ellen didn't care what it took. She'd get her horse back, no matter what. She didn't care if her father noticed she'd gone missing. Let him do his worst upon her return, if he hadn't already gotten his fill earlier at dinner.

Hiking up her skirts, Ellen continued to run, her eyes fixed on the tree line ahead.

CHAPTER 3

Douglas Campbell glided through the trees like a ghost. He knew these woods inside and out. Every twist, every tree, every overturned log, every clearing, every stream. It was both a curse and a blessing, since it wasn't as if he'd had a choice. It was either learn it and survive, or give up and surrender.

In hindsight, the night's activities might have been a wee bit reckless. Probably more than a wee bit. But he couldn't help it. Sometimes he could tamp down the rage always simmering somewhere beneath his skin. But sometimes it grew too hot, and he couldn't resist the burn, couldn't douse the flames intent on boiling him alive unless he found an outlet and did something about it.

Lord Bryan. *Lord Bryan.* Just the name set his lips curling back into a snarl. The English noble living in that castle on *his* lands. His horses living in the stable that should be *his.* Well, not anymore, Douglas amended, with a self-satisfied smirk.

He didn't know how long it would take to round up the horses he'd set free, but he hoped it would be several days. Or best yet, that they'd lose half of them. It wasn't a quarter of what the man deserved to lose, but Douglas had long since accepted that he would take what he could get, no matter how small the retaliation, until the day for his ultimate revenge came at last.

Because one day, *one day,* he'd drive that man, his army of servants, and his puffed-up daughter, out of that castle and off his lands for good. He'd reinstate the Campbell clan where it belonged. The First War for Scottish Independence might not have gone in their favour, but he'd fight it again, and again, and again, until it did. Hell, he'd *start* the next war if that was it took to defeat English rule once and for all and reclaim his home.

In the meantime, however, he had to lay low, which was not exactly his best skill. He'd been forced to adapt though, considering the price on his head. Wanted for treason against the Crown. He rolled his eyes up at the heavens at the thought and wanted to scream. The irony, the injustice, *rankled* within him. Never would he forget that God-awful day when Lord Bryan stormed his land and home and took possession. Douglas and his men hadn't stood a chance. And then *he*, Douglas Campbell, was accused of treason. The only thing that kept him going were the small acts of stolen rebellion he managed to carry out against the hateful Lord Bryan, and the fact that one day he wouldn't be a fugitive anymore.

No more living in exile, no more years spent memorizing the woods, hunkering in the shadows, and watching his enemy infiltrate his home while he was sentenced to a seaside existence, carving a makeshift home out of a coastal cave, where he'd been for years now. It was primitive at best, and he didn't care that he'd conquered the lifestyle. It wasn't the victory he wanted. But one day, he'd get what he dreamed of, and he couldn't wait to watch Lord Bryan burn.

Clearing the trees, he reached the coast at last. Craggy cliffs jutted out over the waves crashing against the rocks below. His feet found the treacherous path carved into the side of the cliff, and he followed its winding trail down to his cave. He could walk its curves with his eyes closed at that point, despite the lethal drop to the rocks directly below.

Three quarters of the way down to the pebbled shore, Douglas swung into his cave. He'd done the best he could with it; he'd even created a semblance of two rooms. A larger living area, combined with a crudely-styled kitchen, was situated at the front. Behind it, down a narrow passage, he'd discovered a smaller room, which served as his bedroom. He'd pilfered furniture and supplies from nearby homesteads and farms—only from the English, of course. Not from his own clansmen, all of whom were forced to live on the sparse outskirts of their own lands, where they'd been pushed following the outcome of the First War.

Douglas still blamed himself for its failure, even though he knew it was unfair to do so. He didn't care. He'd been the one who'd encouraged the men, professing confirmation of their impending victory, leading them into every fray with his sword held high, screaming battle cries. They'd followed him, and he'd failed them. Therefore, he considered their loss his fault. But one day he'd make it right. *One day*. That had been his mantra for too long now to measure.

Starting up a fire within the dry confines of his cave, he set up a stolen pot over the flames and began boiling water for a bowl of pottage. He'd been sure to set his makeshift hearth far back from the entrance, where, when the tide was high, the spray from the waves sometimes showered inside.

Earlier that night, he had loaded up some sacks with offerings from Bryan's food provisions before setting fire to his shed. Doing so had felt quite good, and he smiled at the memory of hiding the supplies to fetch them later, *after* he set the fire. Now, he gleefully unloaded the sacks of stolen food onto the waiting shelves. The shelves had been carved by his own hand long ago; he'd made them out of felled trees he'd found in the woods on several of his many forays into their depths upon first arriving at the cave.

Douglas had been more than resourceful with the wood he'd found in abundant supply there. Since setting up camp, in addition to the shelves, he'd carved his own chairs, table, and bed frame. His first attempts turned out rather pitiful, but he liked to think he'd gotten pretty good at it over the years. After all, why not hone the craft? It wasn't like he had anything but time to do so.

The water boiled. He poured in the oats, some honey, and

some milk—all courtesy of the ever-generous Lord Bryan from a few days ago—inside the pot and began to stir. When it was ready, he scooped himself a bowl, also handily self-carved, and sat down at his table to eat. It was nearly dawn; through the mouth of the cave, he watched the sky begin to lighten from indigo to pale pink over the still-dark waves.

Douglas ate mouthfuls of the pottage, but he wasn't really tasting it, despite the welcome addition of the honey. So, he'd freed some horses, stolen some food, set a fire to a house. What good would it do in the end? Bryan would just build a new storage house, acquire new food supplies, and round up his horses, or buy new ones. It was a setback he'd caused, sure—but merely an annoyance, at best. Not a lasting dent in Bryan's regime.

Douglas ground his teeth together. He needed to do *more.* As much as he'd come to enjoy his cave over time, it wasn't home. It was exile, plain and simple, and sometimes his dream of "one day" wasn't enough, and he found himself wondering if it would ever come—if he'd ever restore his clan's fortunes and make things right again.

Silence reigned, except for the lonely splashing of the waves against the rocks below. The sound to his existence for the last several years. What kind of existence was it, really? Time was passing, but it felt as if he were stuck somewhere in the past, and life was moving on without him. Was this all there was for him?

He needed a revolution. He needed something big, something

momentous, to change the tides, to remind him of what he was fighting for, to finally launch his plans for true revenge into action, to—

"*Tilly!*"

The scream split the air somewhere above him. It was loud enough that not even the roar of the waves could drown it out. Douglas was on his feet in seconds. He flew for the mouth of his cave, as the heart-sick scream came again. "Tilly! *Tilly!*"

The accent was unmistakably English.

Jaw set, Douglas slung his cloak back on over his shoulders. He hadn't yet bothered to take off his boots, so that saved him precious time. Double checking that his sword was still strapped to his hip, he leapt back onto the path toward the clifftop, and tore up it to face the intruder. No doubt it was the daughter. He grinned at that.

His fist remained wrapped firmly around the hilt of his sword, ready to draw it. Even if she wasn't Lord Bryan's daughter, she was English, and that made her his enemy, and he didn't care what it would take to make sure she understood that.

CHAPTER 4

It was probably stupid, yelling for her horse atop the cliffs along the coast, but Ellen didn't care. Her voice was hoarse, her throat scraped raw, her eyes puffy and swollen from hopeless tears. She'd been searching for hours; already, the sun was starting to rise. She'd been out nearly half the night and had found nothing.

"Tilly! Tilly, *please!* Where are you, girl, where are you?" Desperation ate at her as she strode up and down the cliff tops, the hem of her nightgown dragging carelessly behind her beneath her cloak. It was mud-splattered and torn from the fallen branches and thorny bushes she'd battled through in the woods. She'd gone off trail about a hundred times, and now her legs and ankles above her boots were cut and scratched to prove it.

"Tilly!" she shouted again, before her voice gave out completely. Her shoulders slumped, and she caved in on herself, the wind blowing off the ocean tearing her hair free from the hasty braid she'd fallen asleep in the night before. The long tendrils whipped around her face, stinging her eyes.

"I dinnae ken who ye're calling, but I can promise ye, she ain't here."

Ellen whirled about, nearly tripping over her skirts as they tangled around her, flapping loudly in the wind. Her gaze latched onto a tall Scotsman standing just feet behind her. She hadn't heard him approach over the roar of the wind and the waves.

Broad-shouldered and distinctly muscled, he stood almost lazily, with his cloak thrown back over one shoulder, exposing the sword holstered at his hip. The fingers of his right hand played over its hilt, almost teasingly. He eyed her through startlingly green eyes; his hair a mass of windblown, reddish gold curls. Stubble covered the straight line of his jaw, lending him a roguish, rugged look.

Her eyes widened, and despite everything, her traitorous heart felt awe before it acknowledged any inkling of fear. She was in the middle of marveling over his appearance, when her brain fit the pieces together, matching him with the silhouette she'd witnessed skulking about the castle grounds.

"You!" she gasped.

Douglas lifted an eyebrow. "I'm sorry, have we met?"

"You freed my father's horses! You freed Tilly! You set fire to our storage house. What are you doing *here*?"

His eyebrow lifted higher. She wondered if he'd already figured out who she was—if he'd known Lord Bryan had a daughter. If he had, he didn't mention it. "I was gonna ask ye the same thing, lass. As for yer claims, I'm afraid ye must be mistaken. I was just enjoyin' some of the finest pottage around when yer unwelcome shouting rudely interrupted the peace of my morning."

Ellen's heart thundered in her ears, but it still wasn't fear she was feeling. The awe over his looks though, that was gone. Now all she could feel was rage.

"How dare you!" she cried. "I saw you from my window. I *saw* you do it! That horse is everything to me—how could you do that to her? Now she's gone, and I can't find her, and I've been looking for hours, and I don't know what to do. I don't know where she's gone, I don't know if I'll ever see her again and—"

To her horror, her voice broke, and more tears welled up behind her eyes. She stopped speaking and spun away from him, her face burning. Furiously, she scrubbed at her wet eyes.

The man was quiet for a long time. He couldn't be much older than she was, she thought. Early twenties, maybe. It didn't matter that he was handsome, she scolded herself, before her heart could betray her mind yet again. *He's a thief, a good-for-nothing ruffian who has cost you Tilly. Who cares what he looks like!*

She fought the urge to sniffle, but eventually she couldn't resist the urge, and the unladylike noise ended the quiet between them. She wrapped her arms around herself and tucked her chin into her chest. She looked pathetic, and childish, she knew, but she couldn't bring herself to face him again. Her cuts burned, her hair was a disheveled mess, her nightgown torn, and inside, her heart ached for her lost horse.

"Bryan's daughter, eh?"

Ellen glared at the ground in front of her. "Yes."

"Ah. I see."

Another silence fell. It occurred to Ellen that she was wasting time. Why was she lingering here anyway? Lifting her head, she summoned her last vestiges of dignity and turned to face him with her chin tilted high. "I will tell my father what I've seen, and that he should come looking for you here. If you know what's good for you, you'll clear out."

She began to march past him, back toward the woods, but his chuckle stopped her.

"Is that so?"

She spun around again, furious. "I don't mean that lightly. If you knew my father at all, if you knew what he was capable of, you'd start running *now*."

There must have been something in her face, a fleeting look of fear, or perhaps the weight of knowing too much, a knowledge that had long since forced her to grow up beyond her years. For as the words left her mouth, it was the first time the man gave up his smirk during their entire exchange. Instead, for just a moment, he regarded her in a new light.

Ellen set her mouth into a hard line, jutting out her chin. Whatever he'd seen in her face, she didn't want his pity. Before she could say anything though, he spoke first.

"I do ken yer father, lass. Lord Bryan and I are well... acquainted, of that I assure ye."

Ellen's defiance faltered for a moment beneath the sudden weight of his gaze and the acid in his voice, and what she could only imagine he was implying. Then she remembered what he'd done, and the chaos he'd caused.

"I don't care," she declared, after too long a pause. "I have a horse to find. You do what you want, but I promise you, I'm sending my father and his men after you. You won't get away with this."

"And if I decide to just stop ye now and be done with it?" The sound of steel leaving a scabbard sang in the air as he drew his sword partway, looking at her with both eyebrows raised in question.

Her own gaze was pinned to the bared blade. Her throat worked as she struggled to swallow. "You wouldn't," she finally breathed, her pulse slamming.

"Wouldn't I?" he asked, his tone thoughtful. He was playing with her, she knew it, but it didn't lessen the fear now finally building inside her.

She took a step back. "My father would kill you."

"Not if I kill him first, aye?" the young Scot said, offering her a grin.

Ellen stared at him with wide eyes. "Please," she whispered. "Please. I just want to find my horse."

His expression gave nothing away. Now she didn't know if he was taunting her for his own amusement, or if he actually meant to run her through with that sword. "After which ye'll run off to dear papa and tell him where to find me?"

She shook her head violently. "No. I won't. I swear it. I won't. *Please.*"

He closed the distance between them. She stayed frozen, rooted to the spot. He let his sword slide back into its scabbard, hilt-deep, and then he reached out and touched her face. She jerked out of his reach, stumbling backwards, her heart racing traitorously.

"Get your hands off me!"

"There's the spirit," he chuckled. "I didn't trust the pathetic act. Ye're fiercer than anyone's ever given ye credit for, aye?"

She stared at him. He stared back, one eyebrow still crooked upwards. Despite the sword at his hip, and his earlier threat, she realized he'd never meant to hurt her. Even now, with him standing so close, tension rippled in the weighted air between them, and she felt her fear melt away. Maybe she didn't need to be scared of him, but she could certainly be *angry* with him.

Gathering all of her strength, she slammed both palms into

his chest and shoved him backwards, away from her. Caught off guard, he stumbled back a step, but only one.

"Don't you dare follow me," she snapped, and then in a whirl of muddied, torn skirts, she marched back into the trees, resisting every urge to look back and see if he would follow. She had no wish to undermine her dramatic exit, which she'd executed rather flawlessly, if she dared say so herself.

"I'll give ye a head start, how's that?" she heard him call after her, the dark amusement in his voice obvious.

Muttering furiously to herself, she lifted her skirts higher so as not to hinder her progress, and lengthened her strides, her head lifted so high her neck began to hurt. She didn't care. She'd show him. *Arrogant, insufferable man,* she thought to herself, grinding her teeth. In moments, the trees had swallowed her, and she left the sea and the Scotsman, far behind.

Or so she hoped. Or *thought* she'd hoped. When, not even an hour later, he showed up again, grinning at her from atop a *tree* of all things, she realized she must have been lying to herself—she could hardly ignore her secret sigh of pleasure at seeing him again.

Not that she planned on ever admitting it.

CHAPTER 5

"What part of *'don't follow me'* didn't you understand?" Ellen snapped, planting her fists on her hips as she glared up at the Scotsman from his perch on a low-hanging branch. How did he even get there without her noticing?

The young man grinned. "What part of *'I'll give ye a head start'* didn't *ye* understand?"

Ellen ground her teeth. "I know you think this is all a big joke, but I don't find it very funny. You set my horse free, and now I can't find her. If she's gone, I'll have you know that you just took away from me the only thing that matters. So please, if you don't mind, *leave me alone*, before you make things worse."

Ellen turned to go. Infuriatingly, he dropped down to the forest floor behind her and used his longer legs to catch up in two strides.

"I'm sorry, lass."

"You don't sound very sorry." She bit off the words.

He was quiet for a moment, walking alongside her. She determinedly did not look at him.

And then he spoke. "Nay, perhaps I'm not very sorry. I was prepared to hate Bryan's daughter, but if ye love a horse that much, maybe I was wrong about ye. And don't fret. If ye mean as much to yer horse as she clearly means to ye, she'll come back to ye."

Ellen didn't answer. He allowed the silence for a while, glancing up at the patches of sky revealed between gaps in the canopy overhead.

"It's gettin' dark," he commented.

"Don't be stupid, it's barely morn—" Ellen cut herself off, because she happened to look skyward too. Without warning, the clear dawn had clouded over with a thick swatch of clouds. Too dark and too heavy to merely call an overcast day. No, a storm was coming.

She pressed her lips into a hard line and kept marching. It didn't matter. A storm wouldn't stop her.

It had apparently stopped the Scotsman. He'd paused behind her. "It's going to storm, lass. Ye need to find cover. Ye need to go home."

"I'm fine."

"Ye'll get lost in these woods if ye keep going like this in bad weather."

"I know these woods perfectly, thank you very much," she said primly, her words edged in steel.

"Doesn't matter how well ye ken them or not. If the storm hits, ye'll be in danger."

She whirled to face him. "I'm not helpless!"

The young man lifted an eyebrow. "Aren't you now?"

Ellen wanted to slap the smirk off his face. "If I'm in any danger, it's *your* fault. The only reason I'm out here in the first place is because of you. So, please, go *away*."

The Scotsman raised his hands in surrender. "Suit yerself."

"Don't follow me," she reminded him, her voice sharp.

He kept his hands up, his expression adopting a mock look of wide-eyed innocence. "Wouldn't think of it."

Her own eyes narrowed, but there was nothing she could do to make sure he kept his word this time. Instead, she turned and marched away. Once she'd lost sight of him around another bend, she did her best to push him to the back of her mind.

Scanning the ground for any telltale hoof prints, she resumed shouting. "Tilly! Tilly!" Whistling for the horse, her determination renewed, she pushed on through the trees, beating her way off trail, most definitely *not* thinking about a certain unruly Scotsman.

Two hours later, that certain unruly Scotsman found her huddled, drenched, against the base of a tree, the hood of her water-logged cloak dragged low over her face. Rain drummed down on the canopy above her, soaking the leaves, the trees, the scattered logs. Mud churned around her, adding to the muck and ruin of her soaked nightgown and cloak. Lightning flashed and thunder clapped, each boom making her flinch.

"Funny findin' ye here, lass."

Ellen looked up, shivering violently. She'd gotten lost. Her woods had betrayed her. She'd ventured so far off trail, growing weaker with hunger and exhaustion by the minute, her brain getting slower and more sluggish, without her awareness. Before she'd known it, she'd had no idea where she was.

She couldn't remember when she'd given up. She didn't know how long she'd been sitting against the base of the tree in this knot of tangled trunks, exposed to the lashing storm, but she did know it had been long enough.

Her teeth clacking together, she looked up at the Scotsman through the blurring torrent of rain. "L-let me g-guess," she pushed out, "you j-just happened t-to be o-out for a s-stroll."

"Lovely weather for it, aye?" he said conversationally, smiling.

At long last, she gave in. Despite her intense shivering, her aching muscles, and hollow stomach, her lips slipped into the tiniest of smiles.

It was enough. His own face split into a wide grin. "Well, come on then, lass. Let's not hog this grand day, eh? Let someone else enjoy the weather for a change while we find some shelter. Dinnae want to get greedy now." He winked. "If I try to carry ye, will ye kick me? I'd rather not be kicked, if that's all right with ye."

"I'll d-do my best t-to refrain."

"There's the spirit." He bent and scooped two arms beneath her, lifting her easily into his arms, despite the added weight of her rain-drenched cloak.

In spite of the cold racking her body, warmth bloomed from the tips of her fingers to her toes as he held her. She was glad he couldn't see her face, because she was probably blushing. Grateful for the valid excuse of exhaustion, she sagged against the broad planes of his chest, and welcomed the promise of strength his arms wrapped securely around her provided.

It was nice. Too nice. She added this to the lengthening list of things she swore she would never be caught admitting aloud.

CHAPTER 6

Douglas tried not to let himself get too distracted by the girl bundled in his arms, but it was proving rather difficult. For so long, his mind had been locked on a single track—getting revenge and reclaiming the Campbell lands from the English. He'd prided himself on his determination. In years, his focus hadn't strayed once. And now here he was, carrying the daughter of the English lord he hated toward safety, and he was altogether too pleased by the circumstances.

He'd planned to hate her. And if he was thinking straight, he *would* hate her, and he would use this unexpected situation to get to Lord Bryan. But he obviously wasn't thinking straight. Instead, he was painfully aware of how she felt in his arms, so soft and yielding. He cursed under his breath. The girl badly needed to get to shelter.

He kept walking. Ellen drifted in and out of sleep as he carried her back to his coastal home. When she was lucid, looking up at him with something akin to wonder in her large, blue eyes, he urged her to rest. He filled his water flask at a certain stream he'd long since mapped out during his time living on the edge of these woods, and helped her to drink whenever she was awake.

When she began to drift off again, she snuggled deeper into his chest. He didn't know if she was aware she was doing it, but far be it from him to discourage her. That would be rather rude, wouldn't it? Look at the poor thing; how dare he deny her some much-needed rest?

They were maybe another twenty minutes from his cave when he heard the voices over the rain and intermittent thunder. English voices, barking orders. Calling a name. *Ellen.*

He froze. They were too close. The noise of the storm, and most likely the girl in his arms, had kept him from noticing until it was too late.

Ellen had gone rigid. She'd heard them too. Jerking her head up, she fought to get down from his arms. He let her go, cursing himself for being in such a vulnerable position. Her stiff legs wobbled beneath her until she found the strength to straighten them.

He didn't know what she planned to do. She turned to face him, her wild eyes taking in his face. He couldn't read the thoughts flying through them. He knew he should be running far, far from there, from *her*, but he hesitated, even as his mind screamed at him to go. What was he thinking?

And yet he remained, staring at her.

She stared back.

The voices were getting closer. Douglas could hear them hacking their way through the woods directly toward them. They had only minutes. Maybe just one.

Douglas looked at her, summoning a steely edge of calm to slow his racing heart. He asked her a single, pointed question. “Do ye want to be found, lass?”

“They’ll find you, too,” she said instead of answering, searching his eyes with a fierce light burning in her own. What she was searching for, he didn’t know, but they were very swiftly running out of time.

Douglas shrugged, feigning a nonchalance he didn’t feel. “Doesn’t mean they’ll catch me.”

She looked at him for another long, hard second, and then glanced over her shoulder. When she looked back, her face was set. “Come on. I know a place.”

He raised his eyebrows. She shot him a hard look, grabbing his hand and wrenching him along behind her as she started to run. “Come on!”

At first too startled to resist, he ran along with her, letting her keep a firm grip on his hand, despite the relentless rain rendering her skin slippery. Eventually, he conceded that he had no other choice but to go with her. He could part with her and probably hide himself much better without her slowing him down, but his heart seemed to be insisting that wasn't an option. His home was too far away—he wouldn't reach it in time, before the search party discovered them.

So, he let her pull him along after her. If she knew a place, it seemed he was just going to have to trust her.

A voice in the back of his head warned that this might be a trap. She was frantic with worry about losing her horse, and she knew full well that he was the cause of that distress, because he'd flat out admitted it to her. Was she leading him somewhere they'd be easily found, so she could turn him over to her father's men and get justice for the havoc he'd wrecked on the castle grounds?

Every well-honed survival instinct was screaming that he leave her. That he get away safely, on his own, just like always. It was how he'd lasted so long in exile, with the Crown's price on his head never getting paid.

But that was just it. On his *own*. Just for once, even if it only lasted a moment, it was so nice not to be alone. He didn't know if he trusted her yet. But he wanted to. And he knew that such a desire may very well turn out to be his downfall.

Right then, though, he found he couldn't quite bring himself to care.

They broke out of the trees at last. The girl, Ellen, hauled him after her down a narrow slope set between two cliffs, toward the sea. He cast a wistful glance in the direction of his cave, but they'd never make it there. It was too far away. He continued with her willingly. His choice had been made.

He followed her down to sea level. Underneath the storming sky, the waves were wild. Crashing, bursting against the rocks. White froth sprayed upwards, joining the rain billowing down.

Ellen ignored all of this. She led him along a rocky, slippery path to a cave. It was too low, Douglas recognized that immediately, but she either didn't appear to notice, or didn't seem to care. She led the way inside. Twisting, dripping columns sank from the stone ceiling arching overhead. As the waves boomed and the thunder howled, the cave echoed mournfully, like a chorus of unseen ghosts hidden behind the strange, sea-eroded stalagmites.

The tide had soaked the rocks making up the cave floor. A pool was growing at the base. The water level would only get higher.

Douglas hesitated at the mouth of the cave, hastily scanning the premises. He was *not* following her in here only to drown if the tide filled the cave, sealing off all escape.

Ellen finally seemed to clue into this fact as well, but it didn't stop her. Scrambling to the back of the cave, her boots slipping on the slick rocks, she climbed up into the entrance of a narrow tunnel he hadn't noticed. "Hurry!" she called to him, her voice joining the echoes filling the cove.

Douglas squared his shoulders. Oh, he'd really lost his mind now. Wading through the water soaking his boots, he followed her up into the tunnel. He had to turn sideways to accommodate the generous breadth of his shoulders.

The deeper they went into the cave, the quieter it became. Soon, even the thunder and cry of the raging sea was muted. He rounded a corner, careful not to brush too close against the craggy walls of the cave, and he suddenly found himself in a narrow space. It was higher off the ground, but he still didn't like the close quarters.

There was a strange glow of light, and he couldn't determine how big of an opening there was, but somehow a sliver of light was getting through. Still, as he continued to assess the situation, there appeared to be no escape except the way they'd come in. They might be completely out of sight and safe from the search party, but the water was still going to rise. He tried to gauge the height of the inner cave with what he knew about the tide, but he wasn't familiar enough with the place to know if it would fill too high with water.

Ellen was climbing up onto a wide ledge at the far end of the tight, circular space. She pulled her knees up to her chest and wrapped her arms around them. He tried to dismiss his growing misgivings. It didn't quite work, but he still made his way toward her, heaving himself up onto the ledge beside her.

His legs dangled off the edge. He leaned his back against the wall. For a while, a heavy silence hung between them.

"Well," he said at last, "this should be entertaining."

CHAPTER 7

For a long time, the silence was awkward. The water below their hanging feet surged and ebbed, providing background noise, but after a while, even that ceased to suffice, and the awkwardness grew. Eventually, Ellen started talking. She hadn't meant to, but at that point, she didn't think she could stand the stretched quiet between them a second longer.

"What's your name?" The question spilled unbidden from her lips. She'd just realized she'd never asked, and he'd never offered.

He paused a moment, as if considering whether or not to tell the truth. "Douglas. Campbell."

That explained the pause. She looked at him, seeing him in a new light, though she didn't know why she was surprised. She knew the name all right, not that she made a point to study all of the men wanted by the Crown. She'd seen the list though, unable to resist her curiosity one particularly boring afternoon that had propelled her to snoop through her father's study while he was locked in a long-winded council meeting with his men and a visiting lord.

She didn't know why she remembered Douglas's name. *Wanted for war crimes,* it had said. She studied Douglas's muscular build and the sword with the well-worn hilt on his hip—yes, she could see it. She wondered what *kind* of war crimes, but she wasn't sure if she wanted to know the answer.

"Ye know my name?" he asked her, looking more amused by her expression than anything.

"Maybe," she said and didn't expand beyond that. She knew she should be wary—he *was* a war criminal after all. But for same strange reason, she didn't feel in any danger sitting there with him. She felt more danger being in the same room with her father.

"Well, will ye return the favour?"

She frowned at him. "What?"

"Yer name. I gave ye mine—including the price on it and everythin'. Seems only fair." A smile played at the corners of his lips.

She flushed. "Oh. Right. It's Ellen. Ellen Bryan, but you already knew that."

"Aye, I did," he replied, studying her too closely for her liking. She looked away, at the rushing water below their ledge. Was it just her, or was the water rising?

"Well, are ye goin' to ask why I've got a price on my head or not?"

She pulled her gaze from the frothing waves and stared at him. "I beg your pardon?"

"Dinnae hide behind your uppity English manners. We all ken ye better than that."

Her cheeks grew hot. "I am *not* uppi—" She broke off when she realized he was laughing at her. Blowing out an annoyed breath, she drew upon the last of her dignity. "I didn't want to impose."

He snorted. "Ye're doin' it again. Dinnae lie. Ye want to ask."

"Of course, I do!" she exploded. "But I also *don't*, because I'd rather not learn I'm trapped inside a cave with a murderous traitor when I can't exactly escape any time soon."

He continued to grin. "I'm not a murderous traitor."

Some of the tension leaked from her shoulders. "No?" she asked, unable to hide the hopefulness in her tone.

"Not a *traitor* anyway." His grin dominated his face.

She jabbed him in the side, hard, with her elbow. "You are *insufferable!*"

"Careful now, lassie, you dinnae want to anger a murderous Scotsman. Won't bode well for ye."

She shot him a glare. "Would you stop? Why are you *actually* wanted by the Crown? What crime did you commit? Although, I fear I already know."

His grin faded. He turned his gaze to the opposite wall of the narrow cave, but Ellen didn't think he was looking at it. No, he was looking inward, at something only he could see. At long last, he started to speak.

"It was war," he said with a slow shrug. "Our homes were being taken over by the English. Wc had to defend them. I fought alongside some of the greatest men Scotland has ever known. I fought for my lands, for my clan, for my people. And I lost. All of it. My clansmen are destitute, scattered to the wind, I've been living in a cave for the last years, and my *home* is currently inhabited by an Englishman. The same Englishman who has the gall to call *me* the traitor." He spat out the last sentence, and Ellen felt her stomach curdle.

"I—I didn't know," she said finally. "I'm sorry, Douglas." Just when she thought she couldn't dislike her father any more than she already did.

Douglas appeared to shake away the anger, and it melted off him as quickly as it had come. "Aye," he muttered. "Well, it's not yer fault, lass."

It went without saying exactly whose fault it was. They both knew it, but neither said it aloud. Ellen had begun thinking that now that they were talking, the awkwardness between them couldn't get any worse. She'd been wrong. She sighed inwardly.

"It's not over though," he continued, suddenly. "Maybe the battle that cost me the Campbell lands has ended, but the war isn't done yet. My country isn't free yet, Ellen. And I can't rest, I can't settle, I can't even have a normal life until it is. Scotland *will* have independence one day, mark my words."

Disquiet settled in Ellen's soul. She licked her lips nervously, glancing over at him. "You believe that?"

"I *ken* that," he corrected, the passion returning to his voice. "I'll make it happen, too, if I have to start and finish the war by myself."

Ellen tried to keep quiet. She really did. She could sense the fervor aflame beneath his skin, and she knew she shouldn't test it. So, they'd exchanged names, he'd saved her life, and she'd saved his. They were still strangers. He was still a wanted criminal, and she his enemy's daughter. The circumstances that had brought them together, into this cramped, storm-ridden cave were tenuous at best. He hadn't asked for her opinion. *So don't give it, you fool,* the voice in the back of her head pleaded. As usual, Ellen ignored the warning.

"Why does it have to be war?" she asked at last, wrapping her arms around her middle. She should really take off her sopping cloak. It wasn't helping to ease her shivers in the slightest. "Why can't it be peace?"

Douglas barked a laugh lacking humour. "Peace? *Peace?* And how do ye propose *that* will solve anything, lass? Are ye mad?"

Ellen's face coloured. "I just—I just thought that maybe if we weren't always resorting to violence, good things could actually start to happen."

"In *what* world, lass?"

"Well, preferably this one, if we could get ourselves together and learn how to *live* side-by-side."

"That won't happen until we Scots have independence."

"Why?" she exploded. "Why do we need to label it? Why can't we just *be*? Live alongside one another without constantly going for each other's throats. Share the land without killing for it. You're outnumbered, Douglas. You said it yourself—your clan is scattered, and that if you want a war, you might just have to start it yourself, which by the way, is the stupidest thing I have ever heard. So maybe if you'd stop and think for a second, you could come up with a better way to reinstate your clan and return to your home. A *peaceful* way."

"Oh, aye, so I'm expected to just waltz up to the castle and kindly ask yer brute of a father to leave? I'm sure that'll go over well. Will ye do me the honour of burying my headless body, or shall I locate a friend to perform that holy task instead?"

Embarrassment gave way to defiance. "I didn't say that!" she snapped.

"Well then, enlighten me. What did ye mean?" He adopted a look of patience, but she knew it was feigned, his jaw tensed beneath the façade, and so she glared at him.

“I don’t know yet. I haven’t given it much thought. If you haven’t noticed, I’m wet, I’m freezing, we’re very possibly in danger of drowning, and if not drowning, then starvation. So, if you don’t mind, I’d prefer to save the war talk for a more convenient opportunity.”

Now they were both glaring at one another. Ellen was trying to maintain the air of righteous defiance she rather felt she’d mastered with that last argument, but it was steadily dissolving the longer she looked at him, because he was so irritatingly handsome that it was distracting.

Douglas also seemed to be losing steam, but considering how Ellen could only begin to imagine how disheveled she must look, she didn’t think it was quite for the same reason on his part.

“Aye,” he said finally. “Perhaps we’d best make an effort to get warm, seeing as we don’t know how long we’ll be stuck here.”

He cast a glance at the water filling the cave. She focused on his expression, trying to read his gauge on the situation—if it was dire, she had a feeling he wouldn’t tell her—but his face gave nothing away. At last, he looked back at her. “All right, lass. Nothing else for it. Tell me, what’s more important to ye—survival or modesty?”

CHAPTER 8

Several minutes later, they were huddled together beneath Douglas's larger cloak in nothing but their underthings. Ellen's face had to be bright red, her cheeks and neck so hot that she was certain if the blush would share its heat with the rest of her body, this extreme survival tactic would not be necessary.

Not that she was complaining. *Still.* She could feel the muscles of his arm pressed against hers, his forearm warm against the exposed skin of her midriff. It was *mortifying*, and yet—well, also thrilling, if she were being honest.

She risked a sideways glance at him when she thought he wasn't looking. Her eyes travelled over his cheekbones, his jawline, the slope of his nose. Her heart beat faster when she realized he just might be the most beautiful man she had ever seen. As far as storybook heroes went, he more than fit the part of everything she'd ever dreamed of—his presence in the adventure she'd always imagined for her future would be quite complimentary, she rather thought.

Except for the part where he's a wanted criminal who has sworn revenge on your father, a snide voice reminded her.

She scowled. It was at this moment that Douglas chose to look over at her. She hastened to correct her expression, but only succeeded in flushing what she was sure was a deeper shade of scarlet. Hurriedly, she turned away, staring instead at one of the jagged rocks protruding from the wall of the side of the cave.

She knew his eyes remained on her bare shoulder that protruded from the cloak. The slightly-transparent, linen shift she was still wearing didn't leave much to the imagination, and she was well aware of this. She pictured her shoulder burning beneath the weight of his gaze. Her skin twitched as if she had an itch. She tried to focus instead on the rising water level—*you can almost reasonably call this a death experience, Ellen, so* stop *thinking about the man beside you, and perhaps concentrate instead on how to get out of here alive.*

Her inner voice, however correct, unfortunately only came off as background noise. The heat radiating off the aforementioned man beside her was too distracting to pay attention to petty things like rising tide levels and potentially fatal situations.

"We'll be all right, if that's what ye're wonderin'," Douglas said suddenly. "We're safe up on this ledge."

"Are you saying that to make me feel better, or because it's true?"

"Both," Douglas offered, shrugging.

Ellen narrowed her eyes, looking at him. She judged that she'd gotten her expression and colouring somewhat back under control. Or so she hoped. "Which is it, Douglas Campbell?"

A smile tugged at the corner of his lips. "More the former, if I'm bein' honest. I dinnae ken this cave. But all things considered, I can think of worse ways to die."

Ellen stared at him, her face was flaming again. She couldn't quite seem to look away this time. "Do you always use humour to deflect fear, or is this a new tactic you are testing out strictly for our current situation?"

Even as the words left her mouth, she didn't know why she bothered—even if what he'd said was a joke, she couldn't help but agree with him.

He shrugged carelessly. "Does it matter?"

She narrowed her eyes again. "And the fact that you'd be dying alongside an Englishwoman, representative of the people you hate?"

Surprise touched his eyes, as if he hadn't considered she'd ever dare ask the question. It was his answer, though, that surprised her. "I have a feeling ye're not like the rest," he said quietly, at last.

"How?" she challenged, not sure why she was pressing it but

unable to stem her curiosity. Even before he answered, her heart quickened in her chest, until she was certain he could hear it pounding.

He held her gaze in his. "Ye're different, Ellen. Ye're not yer father, for one thing. That much is clear. And ... well, I like ye. Maybe I barely ken ye, but I ken that much. So, to answer your question, it'd be an honour to die alongside ye, Miss Ellen Bryan."

Ellen stared at him. He stared back. The air crackled with tension between them. She hardly dared to breathe, in case she'd disturb whatever it was that suddenly branched between them, connecting them in some sudden, inexplicable way she couldn't yet comprehend.

It was a long time before either of them noticed the water level was no longer rising, but rather sinking. When this became apparent, they traded looks. Ellen bit her lip. How stupid was it that she was almost disappointed—and how much more stupid was it that it almost seemed as if he was, too? Once the water ebbed enough, they'd be free to go. For a while, it was nice to be trapped there with him. Actually, it was more like the rest of the world had been trapped outside, and they were safe from its intrusive reality, which was already imposing on their tiny oasis, the more the water levels dropped.

Douglas shifted slightly. Ellen ducked her head, already moving to gather her clothes. They were still damp, but there was no way she was going home in this state of undress.

"Well," she said finally, reluctantly. "I guess ... I guess we should get going."

"Right," he said, not moving.

She swallowed. "My father will be upset. He isn't ... he isn't a nice man. I need to get back."

Isn't a nice man was a stretch, but she didn't feel like going into detail about her relationship with her father. But if anything could break whatever spell had been cast upon them inside this cave, it was the mention of Lord Bryan.

Sure enough, Douglas's face darkened. "Why? Why go back?"

She turned to stare at him. "*Why?* It's home, Douglas. I have to."

He shook his head. "Nay. Ye dinnae have to. Come back with me instead."

She looked at him with wide eyes. "What?" she whispered.

His face was alight with passion. "I'm serious, lass. The man's a tyrant, and ye've as good as admitted it yerself. Come back with me. Maybe..." He paused, and then squared his shoulders, resolutely meeting her gaze. "Maybe we can further discuss this 'peaceful' unity ye were so fond of telling me about before."

Ellen searched his eyes, with wonder spelled out in hers. She wanted to go with him. More than anything, she wanted to shout yes and throw herself in his arms like a proper romantic heroine would. Except ... he *was* wanted by the Crown. He *was* her father's enemy. And she'd only known him a handful of hours. She had to go home. She had to see if Tilly had been found. She had to appease her father for a little while at least, and then maybe ... maybe go from there. Find Douglas Campbell again.

Judging by the way his face fell, he could see her answer in her eyes even before she opened her mouth. She clenched her teeth, hating herself even as she said it, "I'm sorry, Douglas. But I have to go home."

He didn't argue, no matter how much he might have wanted to. Once the water had lowered enough for them to leave the cave, they dressed in silence.

Ellen kept stealing glances at his turned back. She couldn't rid herself of the unsettled feeling that had sunk into her gut the moment she'd turned down his offer. And yet, she also couldn't go back on her answer.

It was disappointing to finally admit, for the first time in her life, that perhaps she was more practical than she'd always believed, after all.

CHAPTER 9

They'd been walking about a half hour by the time Douglas brought the subject back up. She'd been waiting for it; she might not have known him longer than a day, but it wasn't hard to deduce that Douglas Campbell was not a man to let things go easily.

"Wait, Ellen. Just a wee moment. Talk to me. Are ye sure I can't change yer mind?"

A few paces ahead of him, she briefly closed her eyes, and before turning to face him, she willed herself to be strong, to *not* give into temptation and grant him any desire he wished.

They were deep in the forest at this point. The storm had abated. The sky was still overcast and heavy with clouds, but at least they were no longer threatening, just depressing. The grass underfoot was spongy, but since Ellen's boots and stockings were still damp, she hardly noticed.

They'd stopped in the clearing with the small waterfall she often visited with Tilly. A fist closed over her heart at the thought of her horse. Her throat tightening, she tried to dismiss the fears that had been multiplying the closer they got to the castle grounds. What if Tilly wasn't back? What if they hadn't found her? The only conclusion then would be that she was long gone, or that she'd been snapped up by a new owner, who wouldn't miss the opportunity to capture a lost horse free of charge. The fist squeezed tighter around her heart as her thoughts raced.

Water splashed from the pile of rocks built into the steep slope, tinkling down to the pond below. Ellen wished it were a normal day. She wished she were there with Tilly, the horse cheerfully munching away at the grass along the banks, while she sat atop her favourite rock, staring up at the sky through the breaks in the branches daydreaming of ... well. Daydreaming of exactly the situation she was in now, give or take some uglier details.

Ellen's cheeks flushed. What was wrong with her? Here she was, caught up unexpectedly with an extremely handsome man who for some reason kept trying to keep her around—in other words, *her dream come true*—and she was wishing things could go back to *normal?* She wanted to bury her face in her hands and scream, miserable with herself. It was one thing not to understand other people, but to not understand *yourself?* She moaned inwardly.

"I have to go home, Douglas. I told you. I'm sorry." She made herself meet his eyes, even though it would have been easier to stare at her feet instead.

He took a step closer to her. "I told ye we could discuss yer idea for peace or—"

Ellen couldn't help it. She threw her hands in the air, a helpless expression taking over her face. "Douglas, you and I both know that's not an option. Not for you. Admit it. I don't even know why I tried to suggest it."

He frowned. "What do ye—"

She sighed. "Maybe I've just met you, but you told me yourself that you've held onto the idea of revenge for so long. You aren't just going to let it go, simply because you've met me and I asked nicely for you to think of a different way. That's now how it works for you. I know that. So, please, don't insult my intelligence by pretending it's an option in order to get me to come with you."

Douglas glared at her. "I'm not tryin' to—to *trick* ye, lass!" he exclaimed. "I meant it, I'm willin' to talk, to think it—"

"It won't work!" Ellen broke in, unable to explain her sudden frustration. "Maybe you genuinely want it to, but it won't. Deep down, you know it. You'll never get my father out of the castle and off your lands, so I don't even know why you're bothering to try."

Douglas opened his mouth, but no sound came out. He looked as if she'd struck him.

Ellen's shoulders dropped. "I'm sorry," she said, hating herself. She finally gave in and broke eye contact, looking at his boots instead. "That was cruel."

"Don't be sorry," Douglas said, surprising her, his voice rough. He stepped forward again, toward her. "There's a way. There's always a way. And one day, I'll find it. But right now, I meant what I said. Come home with me, Ellen."

She couldn't believe he was still offering. "Douglas, I already told you—"

"And ye're right! Ye're right. I admit it. Peace won't work. Not for me. I'm sorry, lass, truly I am, but ye're right that I'd never be satisfied. But I can't let you just go back to—to *him*. He doesn't treat ye well, does he? Does he hurt ye?"

Ellen stared at him. Her tongue was trapped; she couldn't respond.

Douglas read the answer in her eyes. His face darkened until it rivaled the boiling storm clouds from before. "Ye can't go back, Ellen. Ye *can't*. Stay with me. Come home with me. We'll fight this together. We'll give yer father what he deserves, and I'll get my home back. Ye'll be free, and *I'll* be free. To reinstate my clan, to reclaim my lands, to gain independence, to have a *life* again. It's my *dream*, lass. Surely ye understand—ye must have dreams, too. Dreams of escape, maybe?"

He knew too much. She couldn't even look at him and see the way he now saw her. She felt naked before him, laid bare beneath that gaze that now suddenly saw too much. He saw her deepest fears, darkest thoughts, secret vulnerabilities. It terrified her. And yet ... at the same time ... it made her feel safe. Made her feel ... worth something. Because he was standing across from her, staring at her, seeing *all* of her, and he wasn't running. He was still there.

She was drifting toward his way of thinking. His passion, his ferocity, it was infectious. She could feel herself getting sucked into the typhoon of energy billowing off him—*except...* Whatever Lord Bryan had done, however he had wronged this man before her, however he had wronged *her*, he was still her father. Dreams of escape and her worst fears aside, she couldn't take sides against him. Not her own blood. She just *couldn't.*

Unless. What if there was another way?

Desperately, she lifted her head to meet Douglas's waiting gaze. Hope resonated with his image in her eyes, and Douglas noticed. His eyes narrowed. "What?"

"What if—what if you came home with *me*?"

He stared at her, struck with disbelief. "*What?* Lass, they'd kill me on sight. Especially if they saw me with ye. They'd think I'd kidnapped ye!"

Ellen waved a hurried, dismissive hand. "No, no—we could figure out a way around that. I'm serious, Douglas. If you came back with me, I could protect you. I could make sure no one hurt you until you had your say. I'd speak on your behalf, tell them they're all wrong about you. I could plead with my father to see sense. I could get him to pardon you. I *could*, I swear it. If you give yourself up and show that you'll cooperate, that you aren't—aren't some savage like they think. I promise—maybe they'll listen when you tell them your concerns about your land, your clan. Maybe peace still *can* be achieved. We can make it work, I know we can. It'll take some time, but there's no reason for this to go to war, not if you—"

"Nay."

"—surrender, with me on your side to—" She abruptly cut off her tirade, only then hearing what he'd said. "What?"

Douglas's eyes were soft with sadness as he gently repeated himself. "Nay, lass. I can't do that."

Ellen felt desperation claw at her soul. "Can't or *won't*?"

"Both."

Hopelessness crashed over her. "But—"

"I don't surrender, lass. I fight. I will not turn myself over to the likes of Lord Bryan, yer father he may be or not. I'm sorry." As Ellen's thoughts raced, frantically trying to find some other way to convince him that would make sense in his mind, he continued, "I envy ye, Ellen."

Temporarily thrown, she glanced at him, startled. "What?"

"I envy ye. Ye're ... not like anyone I've ever met before. The way ye see the world. Ye really believe in peace. Ye really believe it can be found, that two enemies can come together and make things right without violence. Ye're not just saying it. Ye believe the best in people, and no matter what ye've been through—and I have an inkling ye've been through quite a lot, since I ken the man who calls himself yer father—that belief doesn't bend. So, I envy ye. Nay—I *admire* ye. Ye are a remarkable woman, Ellen Bryan, and I really wish I could convince ye not to go back there. They dinnae deserve ye."

For a long time, Ellen was silent, unable to speak. She swallowed hard, several times, but she couldn't quite dislodge the lump that had made its home in her throat. "Douglas, I—" She couldn't find any words to finish the sentence.

"Never ye mind, lass," he said quietly. "Let's just get ye home then. Aye?"

She looked into his eyes, her heart aching in her chest. "Yes," she agreed at long last, and without another word, they fell into step beside each other, walking back into the trees, leaving the peace of the waterfall far behind them.

CHAPTER 10

By the time they reached the edge of the forest, it was dark. Beyond the rolling fields of heather, the castle loomed ahead of them, its imposing silhouette haloed by moonlight.

Ellen slowed to a stop. She put a hand on the trunk of the tree closest to her.

Douglas stopped with her and waited. He sensed she wanted to say something, but he didn't push her to it.

After a long time, she seemed to summon some strength and drew in a deep breath before turning to face him. "If you won't come in with me, you'd best not follow me any closer than here."

Douglas looked at her. He looked at the moonlight highlighting the curve of her cheekbones, her porcelain skin, smudged with dirt as she was. He quite preferred her that way, actually. It made her look *real,* if not even more beautiful.

"Douglas. Are you listening to me?"

He blinked, focusing on her eyes. He realized she was anxious; she kept stealing glances in the direction of the castle. Worried for her father, he'd wager. Well, not *for* him, per se, but *about* him. About what would happen if he spotted her with Douglas. Or was she just worried about what he might to do her after she'd been gone all night and all day with no explanation.

Anger swirled in his gut. He pressed his teeth together and tried not to let his emotions show on his face. What kind of man was he if he just let her run back to a monster like that? He refused to call Lord Bryan a man. Someone who likely deliberately hurt his own daughter deserved no such title. He couldn't let her go back to him, not if it meant Lord Bryan was likely to hurt her some more. He had to try one more time, one more time to get her to come back with him, where it was safe. "Ellen—"

"Don't. Douglas, don't. I know what you're going to say, and I've already given you my answer. More than once, might I add."

Douglas gathered all of his fortitude. "Ellen. Please. Think about it. A wee bit more. Ye ken better than anyone what kind of man he is. Ye and me, we could make a difference. We could change things. Maybe ye're what I've been waitin' for all these years. That opportunity that's been eludin' me all this time. With ye, I could finally—"

"That *opportunity?*" Too late he realized she was staring at him disbelief, shock and hurt warring for prominence in her eyes. "That's all I am to you? An opportunity? Some ... some *divine intervention* to help you get your revenge?"

Douglas blinked. "What? Nay! Nay, Ellen, I didn't mean it like—"

"But you did," she snapped. "I don't want to hear it anymore."

Drawing herself up to her full height, she stuck her chin out at a stubborn angle, her face carefully blank, abruptly masking herself as no more than a stranger to him. Someone he hadn't just been squeezed into a cave with, half-naked, for the better part of the day. Someone he technically barely knew, but felt as if he'd already known for a lifetime.

"Thank you very much, Mr. Campbell," she began, her tone painfully prim, "for your initiative and your bravery, your kindness and resourcefulness. I am indebted to you for saving my life. But it's time for me to take my leave. I wish you well, and I hope that—"

"Nay! Ellen, don't be that way," Douglas broke in, unable to stand this another second.

Her eyebrows shot up. He didn't care. Anger and affront were hardening her jaw, but once again, he didn't care. Instead of backing away, or leaving her alone like she wanted—or pretended she wanted—he stepped forward, took her face roughly in his hands, and kissed her. At first, she went rigid against him, but he was relentless. He didn't let her go, but continued to press his warm lips on hers, his heart beating wildly in his chest, and his entire body suddenly flush with heat like someone had lit a fire under his feet. Nothing mattered right then but Ellen, he'd rather the burn he felt would consume him; he wasn't moving a muscle if it meant letting her go. How often he'd dreamed of this, hoped for this, longed for this kind of love and passion ... and how often he'd had to squash the hope, to push it away and tell himself it wasn't to be. Some people deserved companionship, deserved *love*, but not him. He was made for war instead.

And yet, there he was. And there *she* was, at long last.

There was a pause, a stillness, a frozen moment in time when she let herself kiss him back. She didn't hold off, but rather sank into him like she, too, had been waiting for this, for *him,* all her life. But it was too brief. His defenses were down for the first time in his life, so it was rather shocking when, without warning, she wrestled out of his arms, swung her arm back, and slapped him across the face so hard, his ears rang.

He jolted back a step, stunned. He raised a hand to his stinging cheek. She stood across from him, her chest heaving. Her face was as red as a freshly-plucked tomato.

"How dare you!" she gasped, but she was clearly just flustered, completely thrown off balance, rather than angry.

Douglas couldn't help it. He grinned so wide his cheeks hurt even more than where she'd slapped him. He was in the middle of contemplating stealing another kiss—if she'd let him, of course—when, too late, he heard what his brain had pushed away as temporarily unimportant, seeing as he'd been too preoccupied by the beautiful, surprisingly feisty young woman in front of him to spare any thought for potential oncoming danger.

The voices he'd been blocking coalesced suddenly into an all-out roar. Ellen and Douglas, his smile slipping off his face, whipped around to face the intruders converging on their moment.

It might as well have been an entire army of them—at least fifty men, all clearly Englishmen, surged toward them, swords bared and brandished high. They were a mere minute away.

At first, Douglas was too stunned to move. He'd completely ignored their approach. For the first time in his life, he'd *stopped paying attention.* His heart thundered in his ears. There wasn't enough time. He spun toward Ellen at the same time that she gave him a hard shove in the chest. "Go, Douglas! *Run!*"

He gaped at her in disbelief. "I'm not leavin' ye, lass!"

"You have no choice!" she screamed. "Go! They want you, not me."

He still didn't move, his heart racing. They might be her people, but that apparently hadn't stopped them from hurting her before. He couldn't just leave her. At least, not without giving her something to protect herself with.

Jamming a hand into his sword belt, he yanked out a knife with a wooden handle he'd carved himself. He grabbed her hand and pressed the hilt into it, closing her fingers tightly around it. "Take this," he urged, holding her gaze so she could read the intensity in his eyes. "Take it. Just in case."

She looked at the blade and then back up at him in horror. "What? No! *No.* Douglas, I can't—I can't—"

"Ellen—"

"No!" she exploded. She shoved him away from her, knife and all. He stumbled back a step. She shot a terrified glance over at the men. They were running now. They'd be on them in half a minute. Less.

"They'll kill you, Douglas," she pleaded. "Go. You have to go. *Please*. For me! Do it for me. *Please*!"

It was the desperation in her face that finally propelled his feet to move. He went to her first, though. He threw his arms around her, holding her tight. As he did so, he slipped his knife into the pocket of her cloak. Kissing her roughly on the cheek, his throat suddenly crushed with a barrage of emotion, he wished he could hold her forever, but it was she who shoved him away again.

"*Go!*" Her voice was choked with tears. He knew that this time, he had to listen. Whirling around, he made as if to race back through the trees, but too late noticed that more men were approaching; they'd circled around behind.

Cursing, Douglas tore past Ellen, out of the treeline. He crashed through the heather, the long stalks whipping at his thighs, tangling around his calves. The men flew after him.

Crushed flowers lay strewn in his path as they continued to give chase.

He'd been running only a minute when it struck him that what he was doing went against the very nature of who he was. He was Douglas Campbell! This was *his* land, *his* home, *his* country! These men were the intruders, not him.

He was a Scotsman. He was the Campbell clan leader, and far be it from him to run from a battle. Maybe he was outnumbered beyond count. Maybe he had no hope of getting out of there alive. What did it matter? He'd waited for this all his life. He should have expected nothing less from his cruel life than to have been given Ellen at the same time he must be taken away from her. But that was simply his fate. His destiny. And Campbells didn't run from their destinies. They faced them, and they fought. And if they fell, at least, they fell with dignity.

Douglas whirled around. Planting his feet, he drew his sword. The sound of ringing steel echoed through the night.

The men continued to advance, drawing strength from their numbers. He didn't care. He was ready. *All right, you English devils,* he thought, falling into a battle-ready stance, sword poised in front of him, grip steady. *Come and get me.*

CHAPTER 11

"Lady Bryan. Lady Bryan. Are you all right? Please, did he hurt you? There's a good girl. Come on now."

Ellen swayed on her feet, her eyes squeezed shut. Her heart was hammering in her ears, drowning out the voice of Robert, her father's right-hand man, who had come to see to her needs where she still stood at the edge of the forest, surrounded by the remainder of her father's men, ragged from their battle with a lone Scotsman.

Her world had just been upended. She didn't know how it had happened. It was as if a tree had been upended, and everything had abruptly turned upside down. *Douglas.* Her heart twisted in her chest, and she had to bury a choking cry. The way he'd turned and stood there, his head held high, his sword gleaming in the moonlight, waiting for them.

He had to have known that there was no way he could win against so many foes, but he'd stood his ground and fought anyway. He'd faced his fate with pride and courage, and she couldn't get the image of him out of her head. And the *way* he'd fought... For such a large, strong man he'd moved with such grace and such *speed.* He felled six men before the rest managed to overpower him.

As they'd dragged him away, no doubt to the castle dungeon to be hanged later, he'd looked at her, and bloodied face, sweat-matted hair, wearied muscles, bound hands and all, he'd smiled at her. She'd looked from him to her father's men, the men she supposedly stood alongside, *against* someone like him. But she knew him now. Knew he was someone simply *good* all the way through, right to the heart, unlike her father and the greed, the hunger, and the cruelty her father represented. Something snapped within her. Something changed. Monumentally.

"Lady Bryan. I saw him grab you, saw him manhandle you. I need you to tell me, *now,* if he violated you in any way while he held you captive. We will see he pays for that crime in addition to his many others, of that I assure you. But for now, I must determine whether or not we need to call the doctor, or if you are indeed unharmed. Please look at me, my lady."

Despite his attempt at sounding kind, Robert's frustration and impatience had leaked audibly into his tone, and Ellen wasn't fooled.

She opened her eyes. She looked at the thin, weasel-faced man. Or rather, looked through him, her gaze slightly unfocused. She barely registered the slightly disturbed expression on Robert's face in reaction to this. "Take me to my father," she said, her voice oddly distant, sounding strange even to her own ears. She ignored all of Robert's requests for more information on her capture.

"Yes, my lady," Robert said, managing to hide his concern, or perhaps his suspicion, behind a long-practiced mask of unbiased professionalism. "I'm sure he is eager to see you as well."

He fell into step beside her as she moved through the heather. She felt as if she were in a dream. Her heart was thudding, and her thoughts were fixed on Douglas, wondering if he was all right, if they were torturing him, if she had time to do what needed to be done. She'd better have time. She *had* to have time. All of a sudden, her future, her entire *existence*, teetered upon Douglas's fate. It was a matter of fact now, she could see that. Her fate was irrevocably tied to Douglas's, and she needed to make sure he made it out of this alive so she could tell him that she was wrong, that she'd changed her answer.

They reached the castle. Two liveried footmen opened the massive double doors for her. They swung on oiled hinges. Not a creak sounded. Ellen swept inside, the men scrambling along in her wake. She had a mission now. Deep down, she knew she was terrified, but somehow, she'd managed to detach herself from the emotion. It was too debilitating, and she couldn't risk it interfering with her plan, with what she had to do, because otherwise, she might crumble, and then she'd lose her only hope. She'd lose *Douglas's* only hope.

Ellen's steps on the flagstones echoed around the cavernous hall as they stopped at last in front of her father's study. She didn't wait for Robert to knock and announce her arrival. Ignoring his strangled protest behind her, she grabbed the handles of the doors and pushed them open at once. Stepping inside, she shut them both firmly behind her and turned to face her father.

Lord Bryan stood at the other end of the spacious study. He posed by the lone window, beside his carefully ordered bookshelves. He didn't turn toward her right away; instead, he remained with his hands clasped behind his back, gazing out at the moonlit heather fields bordering the shadowed depths of the forest beyond them.

Ellen pressed her lips into a hard line and waited, wanting him to be the first to speak.

He didn't seem to mind the wait. Once he'd had his fill of the silence, undoubtedly deeming her suitably ill at ease, he spun gracefully on his gleaming boots to look at her.

She could hardly keep the disgust off her face. Everything about him was polished—his oiled-back hair; his elegant buttoned coat that had probably cost twice as much as a servant's yearly wage; his tailored breeches; even his well-honed smirk. He was everything Douglas wasn't—pristinely put together in a way that was almost unnatural, only proving how much stock he put in personal appearance—in other words, in his own narcissism. He was never without that glint of calculating greed in his eyes, as if his every waking moment was spent plotting how best to use every single person at his disposal. He stood tall, his face proud, his shoulders thrown back like he owned the world. But Ellen knew only too well that even if he did own the world, he'd never earned it.

Her eyes strayed to the English flag displayed in full glory on the wall across from the bookshelf. He'd hung it there on their first day in the castle, to a round of applause from the household.

Ellen's lip started to curl. It didn't deserve to be there. Her *father* didn't deserve to be here. Neither did she, or any of their people. It was wrong. Finally, *finally,* she could see it. And it was time her father saw it, too.

Squaring her shoulders, she gathered her courage. To her surprise, it was already right there waiting for her to notice it, right on the surface, perhaps exactly where it had been all along.

She lifted her head and met her father's gaze straight on, something she hadn't been able to do for a very long time, not since she was a little girl and hadn't known any better, hadn't known then to fear this man. Well, it was time to bring back that little girl. It was time to make her father answer for the things he'd done.

Go on then, Father, let me have it, she thought, her heart thundering, but her face remaining composed, wrought from iron. *I'm ready. And I promise, this time you are not.*

CHAPTER 12

"Well, if it isn't my little lamb, back from the wild." Lord Bryan's lips twisted into a degrading sneer. "Tell me, did you enjoy your little rendezvous with the Scottish brute? I saw you from the window here, you know," he said, keeping his tone light and conversational, but she could hear the edge beneath the words. His disgust and his rage were so palpable she could almost taste them. "How romantic. What a kiss."

His lips curled back from his bared teeth. "Look at you," he hissed, his eyes smoldering like hot coals under angry flames. "My daughter, the *whore*. And to a Scottish *dog*, no less."

Ellen's heart slammed against her ribs, harder and faster than before. She clung desperately to the tail end of her courage, but already it was slipping out of her grip. She'd forgotten the coldness of his wrath, the utter terror he inspired without even having to raise his voice. Earlier, when she had foolishly tried to prove her bravery in the face of Douglas's doubt, tried to prove her *loyalty* to her family, she had forgotten just how heartless, how merciless her father truly was.

"He's a hundred thousand times the man you will *ever* be," she finally managed to spit out. She could feel her anger growing, heating, burning through her at an alarming rate. And yet, she didn't care. She didn't care anymore. She'd meant what she'd thought before, no matter how terrifying her father could be, she was ready to face his rage, to bear up under the brutality of it, if that was what it took to save Douglas, his clan, and his home.

Lord Bryan's eyes flashed. He took one step from the window, the snarl twisting his mouth dark with menace. "What did you say to me?"

Ellen also took a step forward. Deep down, she was unable to believe what she was doing—challenging her father, *Lord Bryan*—she didn't even feel her own body anymore, as if something else had taken over, and all she could do was follow along.

"I told you that Douglas Campbell is a hundred thousand times the man you are, have ever been, or ever will be."

She switched direction, striding toward the wall instead, where the English flag was hanging. She didn't hesitate. She didn't even think. Anger and purpose thrumming through her, culminating in an extremely dangerous, reckless combination she was deliberately not acknowledging, she seized the bottom corners of the cloth and with all of her strength, she ripped the flag from the wall and flung it across the room. It landed in a crumpled heap beside her father's enormous mahogany desk.

Heart pounding, breath coming fast, she drew herself up to her tallest height and faced her father, just in time for him to launch himself at her with a roar and backhand her across the face. Her entire body spun with the momentum of the slap—she skidded headlong into the wall, catching herself just in time before she could collapse to the floor. Steadying her shaking knees, she turned again to face him. Her cheek throbbed, and she could already tell her eye would blacken. Right then, she could hardly feel the pain.

Lord Bryan stared at her as if he didn't recognize her. His fury was plain, that much was obvious, but beneath that, as he gazed at the equal rage reflected on her face, coupled with the kind of defiance he'd never once seen from her, a ripple of fear passed through his eyes. She saw it, and drew strength from it, straightening her spine so she stood even taller.

"What did he do to you?" her father finally bellowed, still glaring at her in disbelief. "What spell did he cast over you?"

"He didn't cast a *spell*," she snarled. "He was *kind* to me. It's not a revelation, Father, perhaps if you tried it some time, you might one day understand its merits."

His eyes flashed again. "I am going to kill him, Ellen. My men are preparing the gallows as we speak. His life is over, so if I were you, I'd stop trying to defend the pig. You have one more chance, girl. One more chance to *back away*, to return that flag to its rightful place on my wall, to get on your *knees* and apologize to me, before I string up another rope and decide to kill you too, right beside him." Somewhere in the middle of this speech, his voice began to rise. By the end of it, he was yelling.

"I will *not*," she ground out, keeping her eyes seared to his, her entire body now thundering with her heartbeat. She could hardly think beyond the fear, the adrenaline, the *anger*, rampaging through her. "I will *not* return that flag to the wall. Not until you leave this castle. Not until you return these lands to whom they belong. Not until you *make things right* with Scotland."

"Who are *you*?" her father suddenly shouted, throwing up his arms in utter disbelief. "Who is speaking to me right now? It is certainly not the daughter I raised!"

"The daughter you *raised*?" Ellen heard herself scream back at him. "What daughter did you *raise*, Father? The only daughter here is the one you beat into submission, the one you abused, the one you *sought every opportunity* to hit, to punish, to lock away! I know you blame me for Mother's death, but I never knew her! I didn't ask for her to die giving birth to me, but you still blame me as if it's my fault. I don't even know if you were ever a good man, because as soon as I was old enough to understand, all I could see was a sad, lonely, angry man who craved power in order to have *something* to fill the emptiness within himself."

She couldn't stop. "You *sicken* me! I'd *rather* you killed me than live one more day here with you. One more *hour*. I will *not* put that flag back on the wall, until you make things right with Scotland. But we both know you won't. Because you are a blind, desperate, cruel old man. I hope Scotland gains its independence. I hope it wins the war against you. I'm so glad I met Douglas so I could learn the definition of a great man, a *worthy* man. If the rest of the Scottish people are like him, then I want to fight on their side. I want to fight with people who *deserve* to win. I might not know many things about war or politics, but I do know this: you absolutely do *not* deserve this land."

Her father barked a laugh. It was a horrible sound. Devoid of humour, it tore at Ellen's ear drums and sent chills crawling up her spine.

"Oh, Ellen. *Ellen.* I sicken *you*, do I?" He started advancing toward her.

Despite the adrenaline still pumping through her, lending her courage, she knew it was only acting on borrowed time, and she didn't have much longer before it deserted her all together. She started to back away from him.

Spittle flew across the room as his words left his mouth. "I never wanted you, did you know that? If only I'd convinced your mother to get rid of you before you could be born, but my need for a son was too great. And yet, what did I get? One useless daughter and one dead wife. I have hated you, Ellen. I keep you around only for propriety's sake. But oh, how I longed to lose you, to never lay eyes on you again, you who stole your mother's looks, your mother's bearing, your mother's *life*. I've never loved you, Ellen, which makes this moment a great deal easier than I imagined. Perhaps killing you won't be such a regret after all."

He lengthened his strides. In her haste to back up, Ellen tripped on the ripped hem of her tattered nightgown. She regained her balance only to collide with the door, already at her back. Her father was just steps away, his eyes glowing with a terrifying intensity she'd never seen in them before. A scream gathered in her throat, but her lungs had no air, blocked with panic as they were, so she could only stand there, helpless and horrified, as he approached.

He drew his sword. In the silence of his study, the sound echoed off the stone walls. Ellen spun around and yanked at the handle of the door. She got it open a crack, only for her father to suddenly appear beside her and slam it shut.

He grabbed her and smashed her spine against the door. The door handle jabbed into her ribs and she bit back a cry of pain, staring wide-eyed at Lord Bryan, the man she'd called her father, as he pressed the blade of his sword against her throat. She felt the sharpened edge bite into her skin and knew her blood welled along the polished steel.

Her hands fell limply against her sides. Disbelief choked her. She'd gone numb. She was floating somewhere outside her own body. Maybe she'd brought this on herself, maybe she'd as good as begged him to do this, but just as she'd expected, her courage had abandoned her. She sagged against the door. As she did, she heard an odd clack as something within the folds of her cloak knocking against the wooden door behind her. Her heart skipped a beat. It skipped several beats. Almost of its own accord, her hand slipped into her pocket. Her fingers curled around the hilt of a long-bladed knife.

Douglas.

"I'd say it was nice having you around," her father said softly, smirking, "but I wouldn't want the last words you hear to be a lie. Goodbye, Ellen."

Just before the blade of his sword could cut any deeper into her throat, Ellen stopped thinking. She just acted. Whipping the knife out of her pocket, she let out a high-pitched scream as she drove it right into the center of her father's chest, directly into his heart.

His eyes popped with shock. The blade slid away from her throat as his grip loosened. The sword clattered uselessly to the floor. As she watched, he staggered sideways. His hip hit his desk, and he tried to grab hold of its edge, but missed. Instead, he fell to his knees, blood gurgling on his lips, weakened fingers scrabbling uselessly at the hilt buried in his chest. Eventually, he toppled sidelong, landing with a heavy thud on the crumpled English flag. Soon, enough of his blood had pooled around him that the flag was unrecognizable beneath him. It could've represented any country; no one would've been able to tell the difference.

Trembling and in a frenzied daze, Ellen left her father's study. No one was outside the door. Nausea worked its way up her throat and she had to stop, leaning over a large vase and retching into it. Her hands were shaking. Her whole body was shaking. She was having trouble breathing, but she made herself walk. Even though everything she did seemed to be happening to another person, she kept moving. Her body felt as if it were being operated by someone else entirely.

She prayed no servants would be about. She had blood on her hands, as well as carved into the thin line on her throat, which would no doubt leave a scar, and down the front of her long-since ruined nightgown. She looked horrifying, she knew that distantly, but right then, she couldn't acknowledge it. She couldn't acknowledge much of anything at that point. All she could do was get to the dungeons and get to Douglas.

It was a long walk. And yet, no one was around to stop her. Not even any of her father's men. In her mental haze, she still knew that her luck couldn't hold forever. She had to get to the dungeon quickly.

The guards tried to stop her at the entrance to the cells once she finally reached the damp, dingy depths of the dungeon level of the castle. They took in the sight of the blood on her hands, and looked completely astonished, as if they couldn't reconcile the flighty, dreamy girl they'd watched grow up around the castle with the shaking, shell-shocked, blood-spattered young woman in front of them now.

"Stand aside and then leave me," she finally said, her voice sounding odd, detached, as it came from her cracked lips and raw throat. She hadn't cried. Her eyes were so dry it was almost painful. "Orders from my father."

In the end, the guards let her pass, looking too stunned to do anything else.

Douglas was in the cell at the very end of the row. None of the other cells were occupied. When she appeared before the bars, she just stood there and stared at him.

He was sitting on the ledge built into the wall, which she supposed was meant to serve as a bed. His head was in his hands. Stripped of his sword, he looked like he was missing a piece of himself, but she rather thought she could get used to the sight.

He must have sensed someone standing there, because he looked up. When he saw it was her, his eyes widened. He took in the state of her, and leapt to his feet. “Ellen? *Ellen*? What did he do to ye? What happened? Ellen? Talk to me, lass!”

She shook her head. Her lips trembled. Her heart felt like it was going to splinter apart in her chest.

He grabbed the bars between them. “If he hurt ye, if he *hurt ye,* I swear I’ll kill him, I swear that I will *destroy*—”

“No,” she whispered. Her voice was so quiet, barely audible over his passionate, fierce declaration, but he heard her all the same. He broke off and stared at her. She struggled to swallow, forcing her gaze up from the dirty stone floor to meet his eyes. “He’s dead.”

Douglas gaped at her. He understood immediately, of course, but it wasn’t shock that overtook his expression. Instead, a heavy sadness settled over his features as it became clear how it had come about. "Oh, lass. Oh, Ellen. I'm so sorry."

Her shoulders collapsed. The tears she'd been suppressing suddenly rose to the surface with alarming speed, and before she knew it, she'd crumpled in on herself, the sobs tearing her insides apart as they clawed their way up her throat.

He waited, his face covered with an aching, empathetic look of pain as he gazed at her. When she managed to get herself somewhat back under control, he nodded at the keys hanging on the opposite wall. She scrambled to them and clutched them in her right fist.

"Let me out then, lass," he said softly. "Go on."

She nodded, not trusting herself to speak. Her hands were trembling violently, but she managed to fit the correct key into the lock. She opened his cell door and started to push it slowly open. He grabbed it and forced it the rest of the way open at a much faster rate, striding fto her. He reached out to take her in his arms at the same time that she all but fell against him.

It was only when he pulled her in close, surrounding her with his warmth, that she realized how cold she'd been.

"You brave, foolish woman," he murmured, rocking her back and forth as he would a child. "*My* brave, brave, foolish woman. We must get out of here."

He let her cry into his chest, stroking her hair, holding her up when her knees gave out. When her sobs ran dry, he waited another second or so, and then he set her gently back on her feet.

"Come now," he told her softly, his hands light on her face as he tucked a stray strand of hair behind her ear. "Come back to the cliffs with me, lass. I'll keep ye safe. I'll make ye a home. We're not safe here."

"No." The word carried more strength than any others she'd uttered since reuniting with him. She lifted her head from his chest and looked straight into his eyes. "We *are* home."

He stared at her. She managed a small, tremulous smile. Another tear rolled from her eye. Gently, he brushed it away, gazing at her as realization dawned. "Aye," he murmured at long last, still marvelling over this new revelation. "Aye, we are at that, aren't we?"

She laid her head back against his chest. His arms closed around her, and he held her tight.

CHAPTER 13

Scottish Highlands, Near Loch Awe, July, 1314

"Ah, I should've known I'd find ye in here."

Ellen turned toward her husband with a smile. "You always find me in here."

"Aye, I ken," Douglas said, grinning. He walked down the straw-strewn aisle toward where she stood in front of the last stall, feeding Tilly carrots. The mare nickered affectionately as Douglas reached over to rub her nose. "Hi there, pretty girl. How's it feel to be home?"

The search for Tilly had lasted the better part of a year since Lord Bryan's death was announced, and the castle was reclaimed for the Campbells. The land had also since been rightfully reinstated in the Campbell name, a claim that had been further solidified by the victory at the Battle of

Bannockburn, which had officially helped Scotland achieve independence at last.

Ellen and Douglas had married soon after, but all throughout, Ellen had never stopped searching for her beloved horse. Since Douglas was the one who'd initially freed the horse all those months ago, he'd been searching just as hard as she'd been, using all of his clout as a clan leader to discover the horse's whereabouts.

In the end, it turned out that Tilly had been found that fateful night by a young man of the Campbell clan, living on a farm on the outskirts of what had once been Lord Bryan's stolen territory. He'd kept her safe, taking good care of her, and though he'd at first refused to give her up, once Douglas informed him of what had happened and the moment he saw Tilly with Ellen, even he couldn't deny their bond. He'd let the horse go, back into Ellen's tender care, and Douglas made sure the man was generously compensated for the trouble he'd gone to in caring for his wife's beloved animal.

Ellen gave Tilly a last kiss on the forehead before threading her fingers with Douglas's. They walked out of the stables together. Outside, the sun was just setting over the heather and the forest beyond, the treetops glowing gold beneath the falling light. The old Bryan stronghold, now under Campbell control, was lit up as well, its stones sparkling beneath the sun's last rays.

It was much less intimidating now; Ellen had made sure of that. She'd believed in turning the castle into something beautiful, in the pursuit of banishing its darkest memories and replacing them with hope and light. Bright drapes in Campbell colours now fluttered in the opened windows. A large, newly cultivated garden dotted with wildflowers and planted flowers of all colours and shapes covered a great expanse of the front lawns before the land gave way to the heather fields. Inside the castle, she'd added more light. She'd seen to it that all of the rooms were adorned with the cheerful rugs, paintings, and tapestries. Even the furniture was more inviting, each of the rooms inspiring warmth and welcome for the many visitors, mostly friends and relatives from Douglas's clan, who came by to stay with them.

The study had been completely remade—reorganized and repurposed to accommodate a storage room, but Ellen still didn't go into it. She hoped that one day she would. Someday, she hoped to be able to face her demons and set foot in there without losing sense of herself. She thought that the day might be coming soon.

Every day, Ellen grew stronger; every day, the memory of that night haunted her a little less. She didn't regret what she'd done, as it had been kill or be killed, so she'd done the right thing. She'd done what had to be done, what everyone else had been too frightened to attempt before. Already the world was a better place, a brighter place, ripe with hope for the future of English and Scottish relations, especially with Ellen and Douglas providing a prime example with their flourishing marriage of mixed nationalities. What she'd done was right, but that didn't mean she didn't think of her father often. She wished things could have been different. She wished he'd been a different man, a better man. She prayed for his soul often, for it was all she could do.

Outside in the twilight, Douglas wrapped an arm around her shoulders and hugged her close against his side as they made their way up to the castle. "I love ye, lass," he told her, quite without warning.

She smiled, used to it by now, tipping her head against his shoulder as they walked. "Oh, aye, I ken," she said, teasing him with her terrible attempt at his accent.

He laughed. "We really need to work on that."

She grinned. "Can it wait until later? I'm starving."

"Far be it from me to stand between a woman and her stomach," Douglas professed with all-seriousness, making her laugh as he steered her toward the kitchen. Before they stepped inside, though, she stole one last look behind her, at the sunset painted across the sky. She thought of her dream of sailing away across the sea to find adventure and romance. How ironic that it had found her instead, right there at home.

With her fingers laced through her husband's, she followed Douglas inside, still smiling.

The End

CONTINUE READING...

Thank you for reading ***Highland Enemy!***

Are you wondering what to read next? Why not read ***Highland Imposter?***

Here's a sample for you:

Scotland, Northern Highlands, 1495

Her feet were raw and blistered from walking, but Grizel pushed on. Tor Castle became more prominent with every step, rising from the horizon like a beacon, silhouetted against the impossibly high peaks of Ben Nevis. The mountain had served as Grizel's guide, and after hours of staring up at its imposing rock face, the highest points of which were shrouded in a summery fog, she considered it a traveling companion. A friend, even.

Truly, her only friend in this enemy territory. She was firmly in the land of Clan Cameron.

She was meant to stay behind while her father and brothers went into battle, fighting for Ranald Galda's claim to the chiefship of Clan MacDonald. The Stranger, they called him. *A stranger indeed*, Grizel thought. She'd asked her father repeatedly why Clan Fraser had to be involved in a MacDonald matter.

"Because Hugh Fraser is The Stranger's uncle, and he supports his cause. That means we support it, too," he'd said, his wooly beard tickling her cheek as he pulled Grizel close and kissed her temple.

Her father had always been a loyal man, a dependable man. Someone who placed duty above all else. Grizel had grown up admiring these qualities, and had long tried to imitate them in her own life, but as she'd stood in the doorway next to her mother and watched him disappear amongst the crowd of warriors, she prayed he'd break his word. Turn around, leave a scratchy kiss on her forehead, and sink into his chair at the table for dinner.

Her mother went back inside as soon as the men were hidden beyond the horizon, but Grizel stayed put until the wind no longer carried the men's voices back to her. Until all she could hear was the whisper of the trees.

How Grizel ended up on the battlefield was a mystery even to her. Upon hearing that the Fraser and Gordon forces had successfully taken Castle Tioram, a compulsion stronger than anything Grizel had ever known pulled her toward Inverlochy.

She needed to ensure her family was safe, and she needed to see her father.

Grizel mounted one of the family's horses and took off, her mother shouting protests behind her. However, by the time she reached the castle, the men had gone, headed for home. Feeling foolish, Grizel followed the whispers that the Fraser men had moved in the way of the Great Glen, so that's where she turned.

As she crested a rock outcropping, the silvery waters of Loch Lochy became visible. So too did the battle. Men in Fraser colors wailed as arrows fell from the sky as thick and unavoidable as rain. The glen had turned a horrifying shade of maroon, bright red blood mixing with the muddy ground.

The archers of Clan Cameron were rushing down the hill opposite of Grizel, picking up arrows and relaunching them as they went, while MacDonald warriors waved picks and swords, slicing through men with ease. The Frasers were clearly outnumbered and unprepared. Desperately, Grizel searched for the rest of their forces.

Where is Clan Gordon? she cried inwardly.

An arrow landed in the grass next to her, it's point buried in the soft earth. Soon after, a second found it's home deep in the flank of her horse. Grizel grabbed hold of the arrow, tried to pry it from the horse's side, but the blood dripping from the wound made the shaft so slippery, she couldn't get a good grip on it. Suddenly the horse reared and leapt passed her, heading back the way they'd just come. A third arrow landed in the ground at her feet and Grizel knew she must run, as well.

She sprinted down the hill and toward a cropping of trees, her feet sinking into the soft earth with every step. She could no longer see the battle being waged, but the angry clash of metal and death screams followed her. She huddled in the marshy shadows until she couldn't feel her legs, until the river bubbling next to her ran red with blood, until screaming gave way to cheers and celebration.

Hope flared in her chest. The battle was over. Her father's grizzled face flashed across her mind, and just as she was set to leap from her hiding place and find him, the clomping of hooves stilled her.

"Hendrie thought he saw someone run this way," a tired voice said.

"Oh, let them run," another voice responded. Grizel could tell immediately he was a leader. His tone was sharp and commanding, even in private conversation. "What harm are four Frasers, anyway?"

The two men laughed, and Grizel thought she would be sick.

"Is that all ye think survived, Master William?" the tired man asked. "Four?"

Grizel leaned ever so slightly around the tree at her back, and chanced a peek at the men. The tired one looked like a mouse. Wisps of blond hair barely covered his head, and his entire face pinched into the center like he was constantly smelling something unpleasant. A layer of mud coated everything below his knees, including the bottom few inches of his plaid.

Looming over him was the man on the horse. He was the exact opposite of the mouse in every way. His limbs were thick and long. Grizel could see cords of muscle twist and flex as he adjusted his grip on the horse. Hair fell into his eyes in dark waves, and his broad jaw was stubbled with a beard the same color. Despite the trauma of the day, Grizel couldn't help but find the man handsome. Her cheeks flushed, and she shook her head slightly at her own foolishness. The man spoke, his gruff voice bringing her back to sense, and Grizel returned to her hiding place behind the tree.

"Nay, I doubt if any survived, but the men claim they saw a few Frasers scurry away from the battle. Cowards," the man spit, his voice dripping with disgust. "Either way, they are no threat to us now."

The voices grew fainter until Grizel couldn't hear them anymore. Only then did she allow herself to breathe, and upon breathing, sobs wracked through her chest. *Four Frasers. Four?* What hope was there that her father could be in that number? She remembered his spirit, his courage, and knew with painful certainty that he was dead, as were her brothers. They weren't cowards, and neither was she.

She'd caught a glimpse of the tartan draped across the man's horse; green and red with an embroidered line of yellow. She recognized them as the colors of Clan Cameron, and, thanks to the mousy man, she knew a "Master William" had sat atop the horse. It was what she needed—a focus for her rage, her anguish.

The information had carried her through the night to the base of Ben Nevis, to the door of Tor Castle, to the home of William Cameron. Her father's duty had been to Lord Lovat, but her duty was and always would be to her father. His death required avenging. If the rumors were true, and she hoped to heaven they were, four Frasers survived the battle; however, there was at least one survivor no one knew about, and she was a bigger threat than they could ever imagine.

With a dagger strapped to her hip beneath her tunic, Grizel mounted the stone steps with only one desire: to paint the walls of Tor Castle red with William's blood.

William returned to Tor Castle as the last rays of sunlight gave way to darkness and took to his chambers. A chambermaid had already brought in water for his bath, so he slid almost at once into the tub, glad to have the remnants of battle cleaned from his skin. He'd avoided most of the fighting. Being sixth in line to the throne offered him certain privileges, such as not dying on the front lines. Fighting behind other men bothered him, but his job was to give the orders, not take them. And there was little he could do to change that.

Several years ago, the day's battle would have been a cause for celebration for William, but now all he could think about were the shocked faces of the Fraser men as the arrows began to fall. They had been supremely outnumbered, and their small rank had been no match for the Cameron archers. Still, many good men had been lost that day, and William knew he would have to answer for it. It had been his call, after all, to descend into the marshland to fight the Frasers at Loch Lochy.

The bath water had turned hopelessly brown, so William splashed his face once more and then stepped out to dry off. He still had to report to the court, tell his daring tale of battle and death to the sheltered men and women who lived in the shadow of the castle. Men and women who had never seen a day of fighting in their lives and probably never would. William groaned, but dutifully made his way to the main hall.

Candlelight danced across the stones like sunlight over water, and despite it all, William couldn't help but marvel at the beauty of his home. The smooth floors that glimmered as if they were made of jewels rather than rock, long hallways that shot off in endless directions like the branches of a tree, expansive grounds soaked in moonlight that provided him with a much-needed reprieve from his military duties.

Often, he would escape the walls of the castle and lie in the grass, stare up at the enormity of Ben Nevis and imagine the world tilting and bending around him, folding in on itself until only he and the mountain remained.

The hall was filled to the brim, and William could hear the

flurry of excitement and activity as he neared the double doors. As soon as they opened, however, the room fell to silence. Ewan Cameron sat at the head of the table, which was dotted with large plates of fruit—blackcurrants, apples, and cherries—that no one dared to touch. Every eye was glued to William as he moved through the room and took an empty seat near the head.

"Welcome, William," Ewan said, prompting the rest of the room to mumble their greetings. "I hear the archers I provided made all the difference in the battle today."

William nodded. "Aye, that they did. It was what won the day, I believe. Though, my keen eye for strategy may have played a part."

Ewan laughed and the rest of the listeners joined him until the walls were practically shaking with the force of it. "Our William, always so modest," he quipped to the table. "Go on, tell us how it all transpired."

William relayed the tale to the eager room. How the Earl of Huntly had called for Clan Gordon to split from Lovat and Clan Fraser as they made their voyage home. How men from Clan MacDonald had been following the groups and reported the split to leadership.

"I knew at that point," William said, his words echoing loudly off the stone, "that we would find no better time to strike. So, I urged the MacDonald forces to outflank Lovat and his men. Then, I sent our archers to be the first line of attack. The Frasers dinnae see it coming, I can promise ye that."

Ewan laughed and clapped his hands together, rocking back and forth in his seat.

"Did ye see any of the action?" a nobleman asked, his skin pale despite the relentless summer sun.

"Aye," William said. "I cut down more than a few men who managed to break through the ranks of the archers. By dusk, the field was free of a single living Fraser."

Again, the room erupted in a raucous cheer, and William allowed himself to absorb the glory of it all, if only for a moment.

"Not one survived?" Ewan asked, a fist tucked beneath his chin.

William shrugged. "A dinnae ken. Several men reported seeing Frasers running from the battlefield, but it can't be confirmed."

A nobleman raised a hand to speak, and Ewan nodded in his direction. "There have been rumors of more raids. What's the plan for handling those?"

Ewan waved the man away. "We can't operate under rumors. We need confirmation. In the meantime, William," Ewan said, leaning forward onto his elbows, "we must be on guard for any surviving Frasers. Revenge can be a powerful motivator, no matter how pointless."

It was William's turn to laugh. "The Fraser men are dead, so who does that leave to carry out their revenge? Their wives? Their daughters?"

The crowd roared and cheered, banging fists on the table so fruit rolled from the platters and fell to the floor where it was crushed under stomping feet.

William could feel their excitement in his chest, and he stood to shout above the noise. "I've met no man I couldn't best in battle, so bring on all the Fraser women. I will stand before the approaching horde without an ounce of fear."

Visit Here to Find this Book:

http://lenacochran.weebly.com/books.html

THANKS FOR READING

If you **love Highland Romance**, **Visit Here:**

http://lenacochran.weebly.com/free-story.html

to hear about all **New Lena Cochran Romance Releases!** I will let you know as soon as they become available! You'll also receive a **FREE Highland Scottish Romance Story!**

Thank you, Friends! I appreciate your kind support. You are my motivation. If you enjoyed ***Highland Enemy!*** would you kindly take a couple minutes to leave a positive review on Amazon? It only takes a moment, and positive reviews truly make a difference. Thank you so much! I appreciate it!

Much love,

Lena Cochran

MORE LENA COCHRAN HIGHLAND ROMANCES!

Highland Kidnapping

Ever since she can remember, Lizzie McMillan has been betrothed to Douglas Grant. She doesn't mind; he's nice enough. After their betrothal ceremony, she and Douglas stroll about the garden, listening to the revelers celebrate. Suddenly, they aren't alone. Fergus MacIntosh, an intruder from their enemy Clan, captures Lizzie. Douglas flees back to the village, deserting Lizzie to her fate. Fighting mad, Lizzie tries to escape. When she discovers *why* she was kidnapped, she's horrified at the ramifications. But even worse, Fergus doesn't know that it was she—who at twelve years old—destroyed the course of his life. If he discovers the truth, Lizzie is terrified at what he'll do to her.

Highland Bride

When it comes to a clan battle, Flora MacDougal can best almost any warrior. And her loyalty to the Grant Clan knows no limits. So when her chief asks her to marry their enemy's finest warrior so that she can infiltrate as a spy, she agrees. But Flora finds her skills of warfare woefully lacking when it comes to marriage. Her husband is too appealing, too strong, too good-looking, too ... *everything*. When he sets a trap, she falls right into it. Will he turn her over to be hung for treason?

Highland Escape

Fiona Buchan was captured nine years ago by the Fraser clan and thrust into service. When a fight breaks out in the castle, she escapes, but a sudden snowstorm leaves her stranded. Barely alive, she collapses in front of Duncan's blackhouse. Duncan believes she's a Fraser—his sworn enemy. Fiona escapes as soon as possible, only to find herself once again battling the elements. This time, when Duncan saves her, he finds out who she really is, and they face their common enemy together. A daring plunge into icy waters and a death sentence contrive to kill all hope of their survival. Will sheer love and dogged determination be enough to save them?

Highland Imposter

Grizel Fraser plans to kill William Cameron; it was his orders that caused the death of her father and brothers. She sneaks into Castle Tor as a servant, with her dagger strapped beneath her gown. Waiting for the perfect moment to kill William takes longer than she plans, and things shift. Grizel is horrified to discover she's falling in love with him. When the castle is ambushed, William finds her hidden dagger with clear Fraser markings. Her cover is blown, and her fate is in William's hands—the same hands responsible for the deaths of her family.

http://lenacochran.weebly.com/books.html

LENA COCHRAN

ABOUT THE AUTHOR

Hi, I'm Lena!

I love the world of Scottish Highland Romance! Probably because I've lived in Scotland for the last nine years. When I'm not glued to my computer writing, I enjoy taking long walks with my husband. I also love to spoil my children -- why wait for the grandparents to do it! We have a little malti-poo puppy who provides us with lots of entertainment.

Thank you so much for visiting my site. I hope you love the Scottish Highland Romances I create just for you!

www.lenacochran.weebly.com
authorlenacochran@gmail.com

Printed in Great Britain
by Amazon

65062511R00059